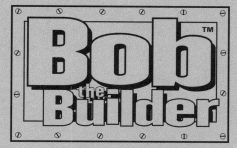

Bob ™ **the Builder**

CBeebies
BBC

Bob's A to Z Activity Book

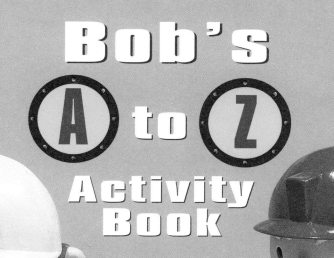

Based upon the television series
Bob the Builder © 2003 HIT Entertainment PLC and Keith Chapman. The Bob the Builder name
and character and the Wendy, Spud, Roley, Muck, Pilchard, Dizzy, Lofty and Scoop characters are
trademarks of HIT Entertainment PLC. Registered in the UK.
With thanks to HOT Animation   www.bobthebuilder.com
First published in 2001 by BBC Worldwide Ltd, Woodlands,
80 Wood Lane, London W12 0TT
This paperback edition published 2003
10 9 8 7 6 5 4 3 2
Text and design © BBC Worldwide Ltd, 2001

CBeebies & logo ™ BBC. © BBC 2002
ISBN 0 563 49111 6
Printed in Hong Kong

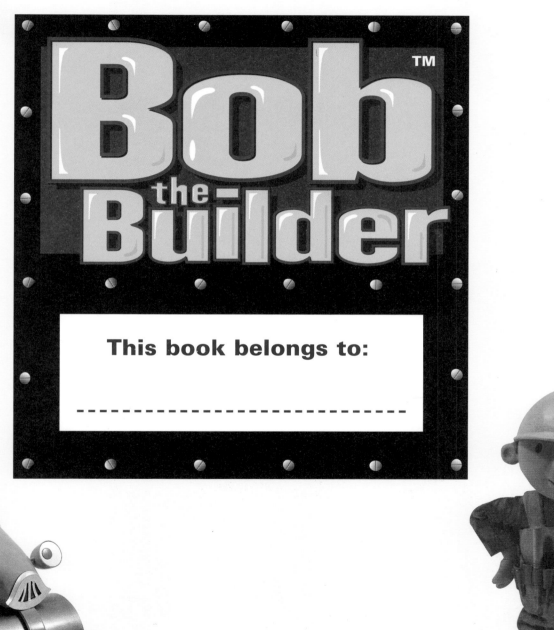

Bob the Builder ™

This book belongs to:

Aa Bb Cc Dd Ee Ff

Gg Hh Ii Jj Kk Ll

Mm Nn Oo Pp Qq

Rr Ss Tt Uu Vv

Ww Xx Yy Zz

Aa

Can you spot the things beginning with a?

armchair

apples

aeroplane

B is for Bob the busy builder...

Bb

bucket

Match the objects to their names.

binoculars

brush

bricks

...and also for Bob
blowing his bugle.

Match the objects to their names.

cake

clipboard

Cc

cone

camera

cloth

candle

CcCcCcCcCcCcCcCcCcCcCcCcCcCcCcC

Dd

D is for Dizzy with ducks in her mixer.

envelopes

eggs

earrings

Match the words to the pictures.

eyes

Ee

Ff

F is for Finn flipping out of his fishtank.

What else on this page begins with f?

green grass

Can you find these things in the picture opposite?

gravel

Gg   Hh

hard hat

hedgehogs   hill

GgHhGgHhGgHhGgHhGgHbG

ice cream

Only one of these three words leads to the right picture. Which one is correct?

ice skating

igloo

Ii

Jj

gjo

ujg

mjup

Use the pictures to help you
unscramble the words.

One of these pictures shows Wendy
doing something beginning with k.
Can you work out which one it is?

Scruffty's house begins with k.
Do you know what it's called?

KkKkKkKkKkKkKkKkKkKkKk

L is for Lofty lifting up logs.

Who's this shy little animal beginning with **m**?

M is for **Muck** who loves being muddy.

mMmMmMmMmMmMmMmMmMmMm

Match the pictures to the words.

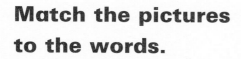

One of them doesn't begin with n. Can you spot it?

Match the words to the pictures.

owl

onions

office

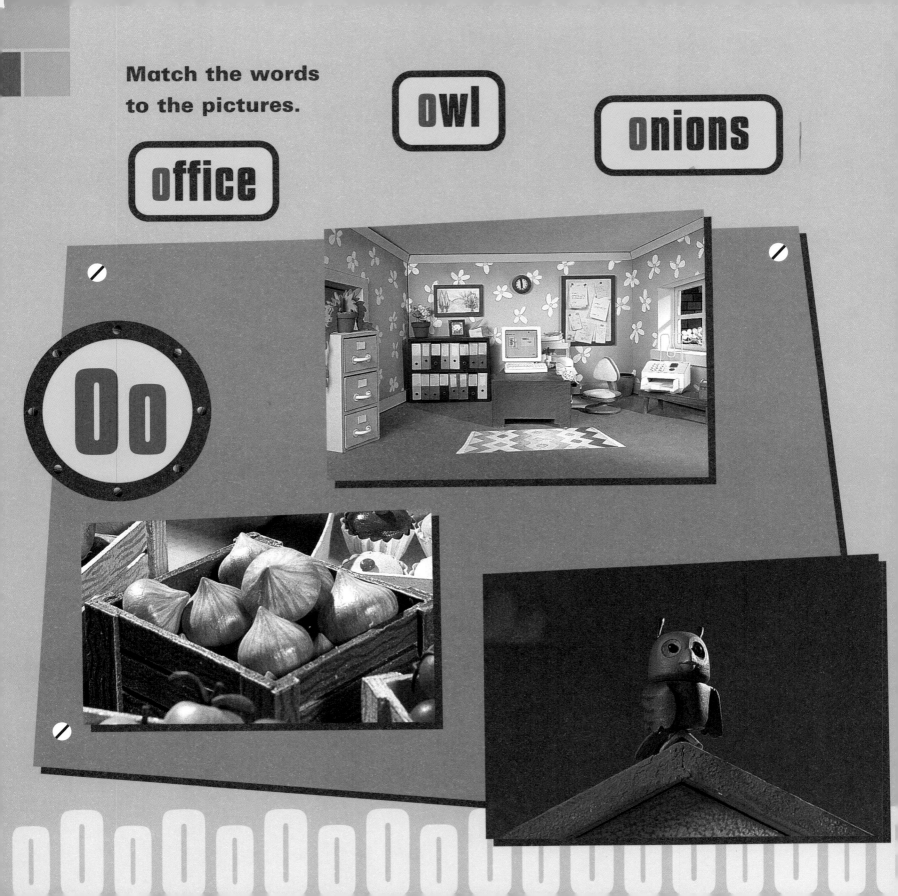

Oo

P is for Pilchard about to pounce.

Pp

The duck on Spud's head is calling to one of its friends, but which one? Follow the dotted line to find out...

Qq

quack!
quack!

R is for Roley
rolling the road flat.

S is for Scoop shovelling snow.

Ss

Which character whose name begins with **S** is being silly?

Tt

T is for Travis
towing his trailer.

Spud is loading up vegetables.

Uu

Vv

This object begins with a **U.**
Can you guess what it is?

Ww

Hidden in the picture is something beginning with **W** which is used for decorating. Can you spot it?

W is for Wendy painting with watercolours.

WWWWWWWWWWWWWW

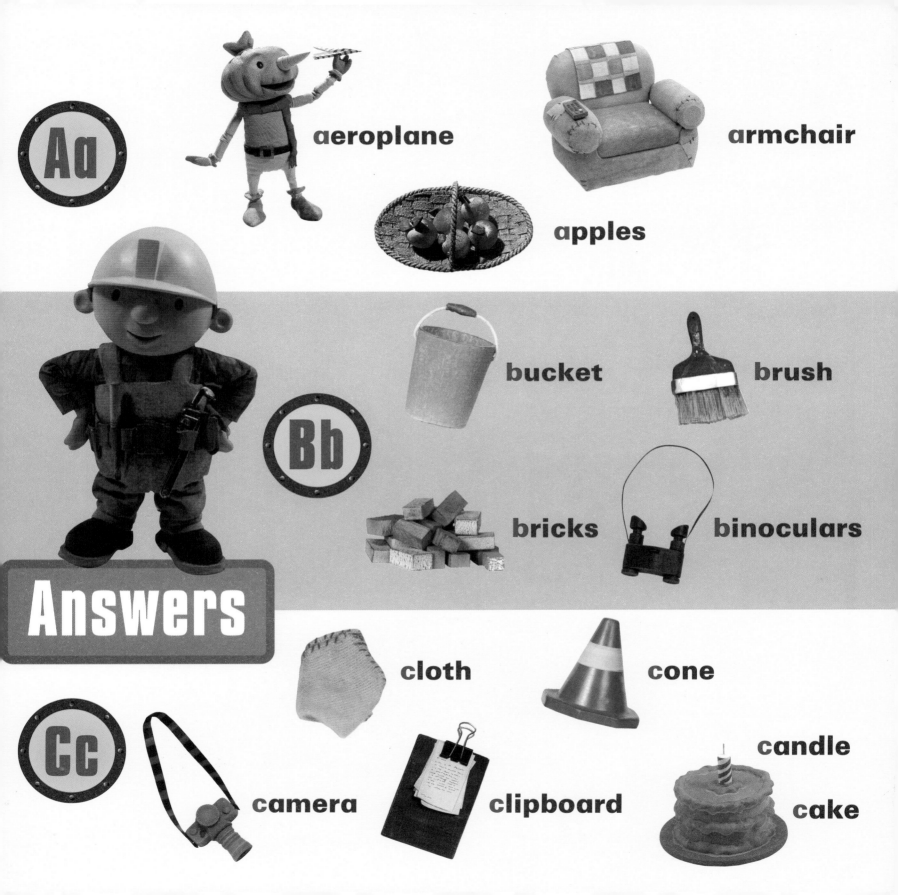

Aa

aeroplane

armchair

apples

Bb

bucket

brush

bricks

binoculars

Answers

cloth

cone

Cc

camera

clipboard

candle

cake

Ee

eggs

eyes

Ff

filing cabinet

fax machine

Gg

Hh

gravel

green grass

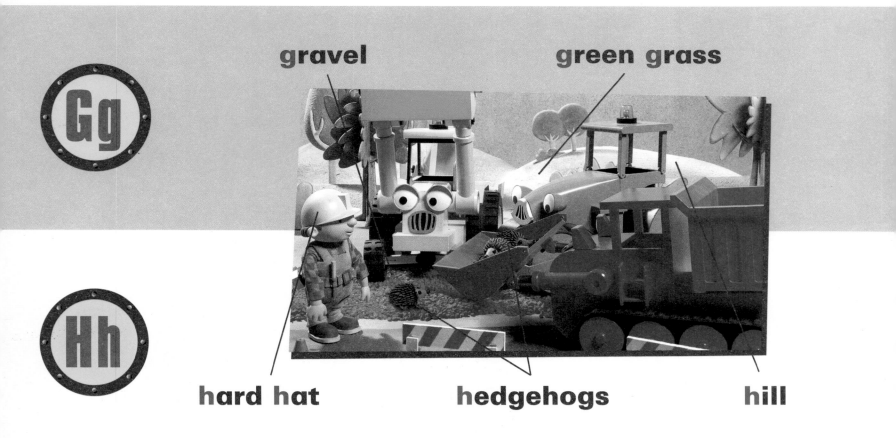

hard hat

hedgehogs

hill

 **envelopes**

 **earrings**

  **ice cream**

  **jog** **jug** **jump**

kick **kennel** **mouse**

Nn newspaper noticeboard nest spade doesn't begin with n

Oo

office onions owl

Qq **Ss** spud

Uu umbrella

Ww wallpaper